BEATRICE
AND THE
LONDON BUS

When your world is imperfect,
there's only one thing left to do:
DREAM!

by Francesca Lombardo

Daily Fairy Tales Ltd.
Beatrice and the London Bus
Children's Book Series - Volume 1

www.beatriceandthelondonbus.co.uk

Published by Daily Fairy Tales Ltd., 2015

www.dailyfairytales.co.uk

Registered address
BEC 101 50 Cambridge Road, Barking, England IG11 8FG
Company number: 09017504

British Library Cataloguing in Publication Data.

A CIP Catalogue record for this book is available from the British Library.

ISBN 978-0-9930433-0-7

MEET THE CHARATERS

The London Bus
(168 via Waterloo)

Pepe

The Annoying
Ugly Fly

Beatrice

Ms Goodenough
(The Mum)

Miss Pruitt

Mr Goodenough
(The Dad)

Mark

The Maps
of the World

The Days
of the Week

Miss Pauline

Mr Cecco

To my nieces Francesca and Emily,
with love.

'Those who don't believe in magic

will never find it.'

—Roald Dahl

Contents

Chapter One

SPELLBOUND

Beatrice looked at herself in the mirror, brushed her hair and put on her favourite hairband.

'I would look very good as a bus driver,' she said proudly. She smiled the way she'd smile if a passenger boarded the bus. If she were a driver, she'd probably make some friends — not like at school.

'Are you ready, Bea?' her mum called from the other room but Beatrice was so lost in her dreams that she didn't hear her.

'Bea, hurry up! Come back down to earth and don't forget to bring your head, please. It's always in the clouds!'

'I am coming, Mum,' Beatrice finally replied, checking herself in the mirror one more time.

Beatrice was strolling down the High Street with her mum when she noticed something nicely displayed in a shop window. She moved closer to get a better look.

'That's the most super-mega-fantastic, galactic-ally beautiful thing on planet earth!' she shrieked, spellbound.

The thing Beatrice was staring at was red, shiny and looked very important. It was a model bus.

'I've never seen a bus like that before. This one looks different!'

Beatrice knew a lot about buses. Unlike most girls of her age she had a real passion for buses and dreamed of being a bus driver.

If only she could drive a bus she could visit many places, explore, see things and talk to passengers. Being stuck at home was boring and, the chance that her dream of becoming a bus driver would come true anytime soon was one in a million.

Plus, her dream made everyone at her school — where most kids wanted to be footballers, ballerinas, film stars, pop stars, astronauts or simply famous — think that she was a bit of an oddball.

Her parents, instead, Mr and Mrs Goodenough, considered her obsession with buses a silly thing.

Beatrice stared at the model bus and noticed a tiny silver tag next to it, which read 168 via Waterloo — *the last Routemaster in the world, who's only friends with the brave and the bold.*

'Route ... Routemaster ... friends with the brave ... and the bold.' The words echoed in Beatrice's head. Then she saw a sign, which read:

A Routemaster Bus is THE BUS beloved by Londoners and tourists alike. It's one of the oldest buses in London and the BEST ONE. There is only ONE left in London — THIS ONE. BUY IT NOW and you'll be the ONLY person in London and in the world to own a ROUTEMASTER BUS.

'I love it!' she gushed. 'Mum, I saw this amazing bus. Can I have it, please?' Beatrice asked her mum who was standing behind her, checking her mobile phone.

'Not again Beatrice! Your obsession with buses doesn't suit a girl like you. Girls should play with girlish things, not buses.'

'Why, Mum?'

'Because all fine, charming young girls are like princesses and, princesses don't get obsessed with buses like you do. You should try to behave like a princess if you want to be a truly fine, charming young girl,' her mum replied, in a screeching voice which made her sound more like a duck scolding a toddler than a grown-up woman speaking to a child.

'What planet is my Mum on? Mars?' she muttered under her breath. 'Mum, I don't want to be charming! Princesses are useless!' she retorted, feeling annoyed as usual by that conversation. 'Why doesn't Andrew have to behave like a princess?'

'Andrew is a boy, dear,' Mrs Goodenough said matter-of-factly.

'I know he's a boy,' she replied scornfully.

Andrew wasn't just a boy — he was Beatrice's brother. He was ten years old and didn't like to play or chat with Beatrice. But just like his sister, he despised princesses, especially the fine and charming ones.

'Leave me alone, Bea. You're as annoying as an ugly fly,' he would snap at her whenever she bothered him with too many questions.

Needless to say, Beatrice was terribly disappointed with her brother. She simply didn't like to be compared to an annoying, ugly fly.

Well, who would?

'Flies are very tiny, annoying and disgusting — I am not!' Beatrice would snap back at him, every time he picked on her.

On the other hand, Beatrice's mum and dad, who as we know, were very serious people, always said that their daughter had too much imagination, and that her head was always in the clouds. The Goodenough family lived in

London — a beautiful, famous city which you will find on the map of the United Kingdom — precisely in an area called Belsize Park.

Like most parents, Beatrice's were very busy with work, chores, bills to pay and all that boring stuff parents generally need to deal with. In their spare time, they loved reading.

You could often find them sitting with their noses buried in magazines, newspapers and sometimes books. They seldom took their children to visit the centre of the city — it was way too crowded for them.

Imagine how disappointing that was for Beatrice. She dreamed of travelling the world, starting her adventurous journey precisely from London — the city where she lived. As it was, life at home was neither fun nor very exciting.

After coming back from the walk in the High Street, Beatrice went straight to speak to her dad. Mr Goodenough was in the lounge sitting in his favourite armchair and reading his favourite newspaper. Mrs Goodenough joined them in the lounge and went to sit on the sofa.

'Dad, do you know how Routemaster buses' engines work?' asked Beatrice.

'Bea, I don't really know. I suppose like all other engines. Your interest in buses is rather peculiar, my dear,' Mr Goodenough replied, distractedly.

'Is our little *annoying, buzzing fly* still talking about buses?' squealed Mrs Goodenough, calling her daughter by what had become Beatrice's official nickname at home.

However, Mrs Goodenough would never

call Beatrice *ugly* because she liked to think of her daughter as a princess. And in her view, princesses were never ugly — annoying maybe but never ugly. 'Stop bothering your Dad, Bea. Can't you see he's reading?' she remarked.

'Oh! What a *dream-flusher*!' Beatrice muttered under her breath. That's how she secretly called her mum.

'Dad, do you think flies and bugs have dreams?' Beatrice insisted.

'Possibly but I couldn't say.'

'Flies and bugs don't have dreams, Bea, and neither should you. Too much day-dreaming is for time-wasters and time-wasters don't get anywhere in life,' preached Mrs Goodenough, breaking into the conversation again. 'And if they don't get anywhere, they become losers. You don't want to be a loser, darling, do you?'

Much to Mrs Goodenough's disappointment, daydreaming was one of Beatrice's favourite pastimes. In truth, it was her favourite one, after buses of course, which explained why Beatrice always had her head in the clouds.

Dreams were *a thrilling and mega galactic- ally fantastic world* — as Beatrice would say — to escape to if someone or something upset her or if life was getting too dull and boring.

If only dreams were a school subject, Beatrice

would have scored the highest marks in London, in the United Kingdom, in the whole world and perhaps even in the universe.

Chapter Two

A PRECIOUS
DREAM LIST

Beatrice had so many dreams that she had lost count of them. Some were big, some were small, some were shy, some were boisterous, some fearless, some fearful, some were braver, and some would even argue with each other and fight.

'Yeah ... yeah ... yeah!' Beatrice muttered, shaking her head. Bored with her mum's endless blabbing, she went to her bedroom, looked at herself in the mirror and said out loud,

'When I grow up, I will make all my dreams come true. And I will be a bus driver! That's for sure! And now, I am going to write down my top five dreams so I won't forget them.' Beatrice picked up her diary and started writing her precious list.

Beatrice's Dreams List TO DO !!!

Dream number 1, I want to be a bus driver.

Dream number 2, I am not sure about this dream — it's a missing dream.

Dream number 3, I want to find a best friend forever.

Dream number 4, I want to go on a talking bus tour of London with a Routemaster bus.

Dream number 5, I want to travel the world ... (with a bus, of course!)

OK, I know what you are thinking now — making all own dreams come true is not easy. Not even grown-ups manage that, or maybe, especially grown-ups. So how was Beatrice going to make them happen?

'They'll happen ... by wishing and thinking about them very much!' Beatrice said out loud. But Beatrice wasn't just a big dreamer — she was also incredibly curious. She liked to ask questions — many questions — and she'd always try to find the answers.

One evening after dinner, when Beatrice's head was clogged up more than usual with dreams and complicated questions, she went to speak to her dad who was in the lounge.

As usual, Mr Goodenough was sitting in his favourite armchair, reading his favourite newspaper: GROWN UPS-DAILY NEWS.

Mrs Goodenough, instead, was sitting on the lounge sofa reading a fashion magazine.

'Dad, what if the river flows but it goes the other way?' asked Beatrice.

'The river flows but it goes the other way? Which river and which way, Bea?'

'Any river, Dad! And any way!'

'I'm not really sure but I don't think a river can flow the other way, it only flows one way — its way,' Mr Goodenough replied, his eyes glued to the newspaper.

'OK, but what if you're stuck in the middle and you can't step away?' she insisted. 'And what if you spend your day hanging in space — what if your tomorrows are like your yesterdays? I mean, what are you supposed to do, Dad?'

'You're stuck ... in the middle ... of ... where, Bea? Mr Goodenough asked sounding puzzled, finally ungluing his eyes from the newspaper to look at his daughter.

'Anywhere!'

'OK — and hanging in ... where ... exactly?'

'In space!'

'Um ... you really have a big imagination, Bea. OK, let me try to give you an answer.' Mr Goodenough was thinking hard. 'If you're *hanging in space*, I don't really have an answer for that I am afraid, but if your *tomorrows are like your yesterdays,* I guess you can try to do something different from what you did yesterday. How about that?'

'OK but Dad, what if everything sucks because your life is so dull and boring? And what—?'

'What ... what ... what! Bea, stop bothering your Dad with these silly questions and stop saying "sucks", please. It's a horrible word and it doesn't suit a princess like you,' preached Mrs Goodenough.

'Mum, I am not a princess!' Beatrice retorted, feeling super annoyed. Mr Goodenough, on the other hand, was becoming more and more interested in the conversation with his daughter. And, he asked,

'Why would your life be boring, Bea? You have lots of nice friends at school and at home, you can play with your brother who's such a fun, lovely and sweet boy. Isn't that true, Andrew?' Mr Goodenough called to his son.

Andrew was in his bedroom, glued to his

favourite video game like a sticker is to a fridge, lost in a world of tanks, machine guns, cluster and bunker bombs, explosions and all the other stuff you will often find in a video game. Not surprisingly, no answer came from Andrew's bedroom.

'I don't, Dad,' said Beatrice. 'I don't have a lot of friends at school! Actually, I don't have any friends at all. My classmates think I am a bit nuts and Andrew never plays with me. He hates me!'

'Does he really hate her?' Mr Goodenough asked his wife.

'Of course he doesn't, darling. Andrew is a very sweet boy,' squeaked Mrs Goodenough.

'Oh, but what if he does? That's not good. Andrew?' Mr Goodenough called his son again. 'Andrew, why do you hate your sister, dear?' But again, no reply came from Andrew's bedroom.

'Oh, well then ... um ... well, if everything—' continued Mr Goodenough thoughtfully as he cleared his voice, ' ... if everything ... um, "sucks", what you really need to do is get out, Bea.'

'OUT? And hang OUT with a London Bus?' Beatrice asked, a big smile on her face.

'Well, I guess that's an option.'

'Yes! I knew it!' exclaimed Beatrice, super happy with her dad's answer.

'Darling, please, do not encourage her in that. It's very bad. Can't you see?' shrieked Mrs Goodenough, staring her husband down. 'You know what she is like, she might take you seriously.'

'Um ... er ... what did I say?' replied Mr Goodenough in a guilty voice.

So, if life at home wasn't much fun for Beatrice, at school it was even worse.

'School sucks!' Beatrice would tell herself every morning when she woke up and every night before she went to bed.

Why? You might wonder. Well, let's say that Beatrice wasn't exactly what you would call a *popular girl.* As we know, she didn't have any friends at school who wanted to hang out or play with her, but the most unbearable thing was that she didn't have that best friend forever — or BFF as she'd say — we all deserve in life and we all dream about. To make things worse some of her classmates had started making fun of her.

'Ha-ha! Bea Goodenough *the bus driver* will never be *good enough* to drive a bus because her arms are too short and because she's not *good enough!* She can't even reach the steering wheel!' a gangly, scrawny boy shouted one morning during break time.

'You are short-short-short-short and you're not *good enough!*' another one cried out.

'Your face is round-round-round like a ball. No! Like a rotten apple! And you're really tiny! You'll never be *good enough* to drive a bus, not even when you grow up. Ha-ha-ha!' a girl sneered at her.

'If you grow up! Ha-ha-ha!' another nasty girl chanted.

'Stop it! You bunch of *mega-boiling-fried stickers*!' Beatrice muttered.

'Ha-ha-ha! What? What did you say? You're not even *good enough* to speak!' the gangly, scrawny boy retorted. Sadly, the teasing went on and on, day after day after day.

This really upset Beatrice, but one day she decided to ignore them. All of them. Yet, she still dreamed of meeting a great friend.

'I wish I could find a BFF who likes buses like me,' she said out loud one gloomy, rainy afternoon while she was doing her homework.

Even though that was one of Beatrice's top dreams — dream number 3, precisely — it was still just a dream.

Would it ever come true? Nobody in London knew but a few days later, something unexpected happened. It was break time at Bell-Bell School — the playground was swarming with screaming kids running around excitedly. Beatrice was sitting on a bench drawing a bus when she noticed a boy standing a little way away, all by himself. He looked lost and lonely — he was new at Bell-Bell School and had not made any friends yet.

The boy was rather small for his age — almost as small as Beatrice. He was shy and had a sweet smile on his face, which wasn't as round as Beatrice's but looked instead very triangular.

Then Beatrice saw the kids who picked on her every day, walking towards the boy in a threatening way.

'Ha-ha-ha! If it's not a *s-s-square*, if it's not

a *c-c-circle* then what is it?' the same nasty, gangly, scrawny kid chanted, faking a stutter.

'It's a *t-t-t-triangle!*' his friends replied in chorus, faking a stutter too.

The boy looked mortified and remained silent. He was too shy to say anything.

'That's enough!' Beatrice said to herself. She put down her diary, took a deep breath, stretched out her shoulders to look a few inches taller and walked up to the nasty kids, defiantly.

'Leave him alone!' she screamed at the top of her lungs, waving her clenched fists in the air. The kids looked at her with a befuddled expression — they had never seen Beatrice reacting so boldly.

'Ha-ha! The tiny-mini-rotten-apple wants to help the ugly, tiny-mini-triangle,' the gangly, scrawny boy sang out while his friends cheered him on. Then he ran off and the mob dissolved. Beatrice was left on her own with the shy boy but none of the two said a word. They stared intently at each other for a long moment until she said,

'Ignore them ... those kids are just some weird *mega-boiling-fried-stickers*. Are you OK?'

'I am, *t-t-thank* you,' the timid boy replied, stuttering heavily. Mark had a problem pronouncing words clearly. He would often get stuck on the first letter. But he'd push and push until finally, the word would come out.

'Cool! My name is Beatrice. I don't like dolls, make up, handbags and all that princess-girlish stuff girls usually like but I do like wearing skirts. What's your name?' she asked enthusiastically.

'*M-M-Mark*,' he replied, blushing. '*I* … *I* … *I* don't like *d-d-dolls*, *h-h-handbags*, *p-p-princess*-girlish stuff either and … *m-m-make up*. But I don't like wearing *s-s-skirts*. Sorry.'

'That's all right — what do you like then?'

'*T-t-trucks*! I like *t-t-trucks*,' he replied enthusiastically, his eyes lighting up. 'I have a *b-big* collection of model *t-t-trucks* at home. I have a fire-fighter truck, a pickup *t-t-truck*, a *c-c-crane* truck, a *b-b-ballast* truck, a *g-g-garbage* truck, a log carrier *t-t-truck*, a *d-d-dump* truck, a *r-r-refrigerator* truck and—' Mark broke off.

Beatrice was looking at the boy with round puzzled eyes. She had no idea there were so many different types of trucks in the world. She only knew about London buses and compared to Mark, she felt she knew very little.

'And what else *d-d-do* you like?' the shy boy asked.

'Buses! I like buses very much,' announced Beatrice with a wide smile.

'*B-b-buses?*'

'Yes, red buses — models of red buses and real red buses too of course, but I don't have any at home. When I grow up, I'd like to be a bus driver — a Routemaster Bus driver, precisely — and repair bus engines.'

'That's really *n-n-nice but* what's a *R-R Routemaster* Bus?' Mark asked, stuttering even more this time.

'It's a bus that looks quite different from the buses you normally see in London. It looks a bit old and has a kind of a round-bumpy shape. It has an entrance at the back with no door, which probably means that when you catch it, you can jump on and off as you like. But I've never seen a bus like that in the streets, only a model in a shop in the High-Street of Belsize Park.'

'Wo-ooah! You know a lot about *b-b-buses*!'

'Yes, I do actually — I also have a very special hairband with real rear-mirrors attached.'

'*R-r-really?*'

'Really, but I don't wear it at school. I am the only one in London — no actually, in the whole world to have this hairband. My teacher Miss Pauline gave it to me last year as a birthday present. You see, she knows I love buses — she's my favourite teacher.'

Mark and Beatrice kept chatting about trucks, buses and many other things when suddenly the bell rang, rudely reminding them that they were at school. It was time to go back, each to their own classrooms.

'I must go Mark — it was super *fantastically* cool chatting with you! See you very soon!'

'It was *s-s-s* ... *f-f-f-* ...' stuttered Mark as he struggled to repeat Beatrice's words. 'It was very *c-c-cool* chatting with you *t-t-too!* See you *s-s-soon*, Beatrice.'

From that day on, every time Beatrice and Mark met in the playground, they played and chatted together.

Mark would bring books full of images of real trucks and buses, which he showed to his new friend, and Beatrice would show him her drawings and stickers of models of buses or she would talk to him about her numerous dreams.

Mark listened to her with a great deal of attention — he liked her very much.

In no time Mark and Beatrice became best friends forever, or BFFs as she liked to say. Astonishingly, dream number 3 had come true.

But despite the excitement of having finally found a BFF, Beatrice was still very much occupied with her favourite pastimes:

BUSES and DREAMS.

Somehow, she couldn't get the model of the Routemaster Bus she had seen in the shop out of her head.

'I wish, I wish ... ' Beatrice said out loud. Countless dreams were hiding up in her head, clogging up her mind and giving her a terrible headache. And nobody, not even her mum with all her blabbing and preaching would have been able to clear her head by *flushing them down* or *away,* as Beatrice would say.

But WAIT! Among that big messy bundle of dreams, Beatrice was just about to find dream number 2 — *the missing dream*!

'I wish ... I could turn that Routemaster model bus from the shop into a big talking bus!' she said out loud. 'This is going to be my dream number 2! The missing dream! I will make this dream come true! That's for sure!' she said to herself before finally falling asleep.

When Beatrice woke up in the morning, she picked up her diary and wrote down dream number 2 — the missing dream.

OK, I know what you're thinking again — Beatrice is really a bit nuts, or an oddball or just a bit weird. She wants to turn the model of a bus into a real bus that can talk! What normal eight-year-old kid who is about to turn nine would think that? Well, let me tell you, that's exactly what dreams are about — making the most fantastic, weird or impossible wishes come true.

However, it's not as if everyone can do that — not at all. To make that happen, first of all you need to have a wish, as that's where dreams come from — secondly, you need to be a little bit nuts, or an oddball or just a bit weird.

Beatrice was certainly this,which was why she could be dead serious about making all her dreams come true. And that's why, somehow, some were astonishingly coming true.

Chapter Three

THE BIRTHDAY PARTY

Beatrice's ninth birthday was just a few days away.

'You'll be eight years old, Bea,' said Mrs Goodenough, 'it's about time you had your very own big birthday party. Dad and I will buy a huge chocolate cake for you and your lovely classmates. How would you like that?'

'Nine, Mum. Yes, I'd love that! Thank you!'

'Of course, darling. Nine.'

But, as we know, apart from Mark, Beatrice didn't have many friends to invite to her big birthday party, yet the idea of a party and a huge chocolate cake was really exciting.

'Um ... I need a trick,' she said to herself, thinking hard. Beatrice squinted her eyes, wrinkled her nose and scratched its tip as she did whenever she was a bit confused or she had an idea.

'There it is! A gigantic cake! Yes, they'll like that! A walloping, stratospherically, super gigantic cake! I am sure they'll come!' she exclaimed in excitement as she looked at the enormous cake she'd just drawn. The cake was smashing through the roof of a house and looked incredibly tall and brown. Then Beatrice wrote down — *LONDON'S BIGGEST CAKE AT BEATRICE'S PARTY! COME ALONG!* She had just come up with a wonderful birthday invitation card. For the rest of the afternoon, Beatrice drew cakes tirelessly and eventually had twenty-eight birthday invitation cards. The next day, in the school playground, holding her precious birthday invitation cards in one hand and waving another card in the air with the other, Beatrice yelled loudly;

'London's biggest cake at Beatrice's birthday party! Come along! Don't miss this great, one-in-a-lifetime chance!'

All the children in her class, even the nasty ones who usually picked on her, hurried over to Beatrice like bees swarming to a honey bun. They had all become super excited at the announcement of a gigantic chocolate cake at a birthday party, even though it was just Beatrice Goodenough's party. They started chanting her name noisily. Everyone was desperately trying to grab an invitation card. Beatrice handed out the cards one by one, feeling proud and important, but kept the last one for Mark because he wasn't at school that day.

AWESOME! The trick has worked! she thought when suddenly, a loud commanding voice resounded from behind her. Everyone ran off leaving Beatrice on her own. What on earth had scared them so much?

She turned around and saw Miss Pruitt, Bell-Bell School's headmistress. The tall woman was towering over the little girl with crossed arms, giving her a suspicious look.

'Beatrice Goodenough!' Miss Pruitt thundered, 'What's going on here? And what are you handing out?'

'My-my birthday invitation card,' Beatrice mumbled shyly, showing the headmistress the only card she had left.

'Hand it over. At once!' Miss Pruitt ordered, growling. Looking at the drawing on the card with a great deal of attention, Miss Pruitt raised her eyebrows so high that her forehead disappeared behind her hairline, as if they had been eaten up and swallowed by a disgusting, gigantic, wriggling worm.

'A cake,' she whispered softly.

Resuming her usual intimidating, incisive commanding voice Miss Pruitt said,

'Go back to your classroom. Right now!' And she walked off with Beatrice's birthday invitation card. Bell-Bell School's headmistress Miss Pruitt was a *tall-and all-skin-and-bone*s woman with a crooked nose, big thick glasses, a pursed mouth, popping eyes and a spine, which bent to one side. No one knew why and no one dared ask. Miss Pruitt was known at Bell-Bell School for her fiery temper — the headmistress had a reputation for being unpredictable and quite moody. But she was also known for her love for cakes. Yet, despite all the cakes she'd wolf down — between three and five a day — Miss Pruitt was so thin that her clothes always looked too big on her. The headmistress also loved cactuses very much but luckily for her and for them, she didn't eat them.

'That card was for Mark,' muttered Beatrice as she walked back to her classroom. 'Never mind, I will tell him when I see him.'

Eager to see and eat London's biggest cake, everyone showed up at Beatrice's birthday party. Mark came along too, of course, but guess who also knocked at her door? The *tall-and-all-skin-and-bones-bent-to-one-side* headmistress, Miss Pruitt.

'Not her,' muttered Beatrice when she saw the scary looking woman.

'Oh! Miss Pruitt, I am so delighted to see you. Thank you for coming. Please do come in,' said Beatrice's mum, impressed by the fact that Bell-Bell School's headmistress had shown up at her daughter's party. Mrs Goodenough rushed immediately to the shop to buy another chocolate cake, just for the very important guest. But despite the unexpected *intruder*, Beatrice was very excited. Everything was going marvellously well at the party and everything was just perfect. Everything but THE CAKE.

'You tricked us, Bea! That's not a gigantic cake!' one of her classmates complained.

'Yes!' echoed a tall girl with a long ponytail. 'It's not gigantic at all! And for sure, it's not London's biggest cake!'

'I'm sorry,' Beatrice said, blushing. *Now they are going to tease me even more*, she thought. However, *the-not-at-all-gigantic-cake* only lasted a few minutes. And in no time the living room turned into a big mess with nobody paying attention to the birthday girl. Beatrice didn't mind too much, so thrilled was she to unwrap all the gifts she had received.

They were all nicely displayed on a little table in a corner of the lounge. Beatrice thanked everyone for the presents and threw herself into the task of unwrapping with a great deal of excitement. But her smile soon turned into a frown.

'That's just girlish princess stuff! Make-up, plush toys, dolls and handbags! Boring!' she muttered, disenchanted. *Why didn't they get me something about buses, like Miss Pauline did last year? That would have been really cool*, she thought. But there was still one present left unopened on the table, which Beatrice hadn't noticed. It was nicely wrapped and had a lovely red ribbon.

'You *f-f-forgot* to open *m-m-mine*,' said Mark as he pointed to the gift.

'Oh! Sorry, Mark! Thank you,' Beatrice replied, looking at him with gloomy eyes.

'Beatrice, I *t-t-think* you'll like this,' he reassured her.

'What is it?' she said jumping, a ray of hope lightening her eyes. 'OK, wait, let me guess ... is it a collection of stickers of the Leyland

Titan Two-door Bus and of the Corgi Bus? Or of the Mercedes Benz Citron G Bus? Or ... a bus driver's cap?' she asked, giving him now a bright-eyed, hopeful look.

'*H-h-hot*, hot! *O-o-open* it!'

Beatrice hastily unwrapped the gift box and spotted a flashy red thing inside. She took it out — her eyes grew as big as two Alpine lakes.

'Mark! It's the Routemaster model bus!' she screamed with excitement. 'The 168 via Waterloo, *the last Routemaster in the*

world, who's only friends with the brave and the bold! The bus with no door at the back that I saw in the shop the other day!'

Mark nodded.

'Thank you, thank you Mark!' Beatrice sang out. She gave him a big hug. Mark blushed, turning as red as a beetroot.

'Would you like to see my Routemaster Bus?' Beatrice went on to ask some of her classmates as she walked around the lounge.

'Bea, toddlers play with bus toys,' mocked one girl called Liz, putting on airs and graces.

'This is not for toddlers Liz! And my bus is not a toy. It's a model of a bus — grown-ups collect models of buses,' Beatrice remarked proudly.

The rest of the kids didn't even bother to look at her precious bus. Miss Pruitt just kept scoffing cake. When the party was over and everyone had left, Beatrice went to her room. She sat on her bed and staring intently at the red model bus, she whispered,

'Oh I wish you could talk, 168 via Waterloo. I wish I could turn you into a real bus, so we could go and travel around London. Me and you. You see, my dream number 1 is to be a bus driver. But how can I make you talk?'

Beatrice squinted her eyes, wrinkled her nose, scratched its tip and stared at the model bus in a deep way.

'I guess I need to cast a spell. Yes! I need a magic song!' she gushed.

It needs to be said that Beatrice had never cast a spell before because she wasn't a wizard and she had never wished to be one. As we know, Beatrice wanted to be a bus driver, but to make that dream come true, she thought it was worth a try. She brought the 168 via Waterloo close to her face, stared at it with even greater intensity and began singing her magic song, which came to her mind there and then,

168 via Waterloo,
the very last Routemaster in the world,
who's only friends
with the brave and the bold.

Give me a sign so I know
that you can talk,
then let's go and visit London,
the city everyone loves.

168 via Waterloo,
take me away from Bell-Bell School,
where all the kids think I am a fool
(apart from Mark for sure)
and they would never believe
I could speak to a Routemaster like you,
(just like I do).

168 via Waterloo,
let's cruise, fly and catch
all the butterflies in the sky,
even the annoying, ugly flies.

168 via Waterloo,
take me all the way through this roof,
so we can fly high and even higher
just me and you
into the sky, coloured with blue.

But the model bus didn't move, didn't grow bigger and even worse, it didn't say a word.

'168 via Waterloo, please talk to me! Please become as big as the red buses in the street,' she begged. 'Please take me around London! The weird and complicated grown-ups say that the streets are dangerous and children shouldn't go there by themselves but if you take me, I'm sure I'll be fine.'

Yet, despite the magic song and the intense wishing, nothing happened. Beatrice took a deep breath and whispered in a dejected voice,

'Goodnight my sweet 168 via Waterloo, *the last Routemaster in the world, who's only friends with the ... brave ... and the ... bold ...'*

Holding the 168 via Waterloo bus tightly to her chest, the magic song still in the air, Beatrice fell into a deep sleep.

Chapter Four

A MYSTERIOUS ENCOUNTER

Nothing much happened in the weeks after the birthday party. But one afternoon after school, Beatrice and her mum went to Caramba Café — a charming little café in the neighbourhood — for a delicious chocolate ice cream. They were now sitting inside the Café —

Mrs Goodenough had her nose buried in a magazine and Beatrice was looking outside when she noticed a big red bus parked in front of the café window.

'Mum, look at that bus.'

'Which bus?' replied Mrs Goodenough as she kept reading the magazine.

'That one, the one parked outside. It looks like my model bus,' Beatrice said, pointing her finger at it.

'All red double-decker buses look like your toy, Bea. They all look the same.'

'It's not a toy, Mum,' Beatrice replied firmly. 'It's a model of a bus. And buses don't all look the same. *This* one has a bumpy look and an entrance at the back with no door just like my model bus. It's the first time I've seen a bus like this in the streets,' explained Beatrice, staring at the bus mesmerised, when something incredibly unusual caught her attention.

'Mum! The bus has just sighed and has moved! It must be bored.'

'Sighed? Oh Bea, don't be silly, double-decker buses don't sigh and don't get bored. You're eight years old and you should know better,' remarked Mrs Goodenough.

'Nine, Mum! Nine and two weeks! And *that* one is a Routemaster Bus, I'm sure of it,' Beatrice replied, still looking intently at the bus.

'Yes of course, darling. Nine,' murmured Mrs Goodenough distractedly.

Beatrice was examining the bus carefully, when she noticed something even more incredible. The bus wasn't just sighing, he was snoring and so loudly that she could hear him through the café window.

'Oh!' Beatrice startled. *Holly Crisps! How did that happen? Could it possibly be that my spell is beginning to work even though I am not a wizard. Or ... am I a wizard?'* No that can't be possible, I am not tall enough to be a wizard, she thought.

'Mum, can we ask the bus to take us for a ride?'

'Bea, a bus doesn't take you for a ride. You catch a certain bus because you know where you want to go, and when you get there, you push the button, the driver stops and you get off. Simple.'

'But that bus doesn't have a driver, Mum,' she insisted. 'I think it just drives itself!' Beatrice wondered how her mum hadn't noticed that.

'You Silly Billy, the driver might have just stepped out for a few minutes. Let me read my magazine, please.'

Beatrice squinted her eyes, wrinkled her nose and scratched its tip. She had an idea!

'I need to go for a wee, Mum,' she announced.

'All right,' mumbled Mrs Goodenough distractedly — her nose still buried in the magazine. Beatrice walked out of the café and stood right in front of the Routemaster bus when she noticed another extraordinary thing — the bus had a mouth, eyebrows, eyes and was wearing a bowler hat.

That's super-weird! How come people don't see that? Summing up all her courage, she decided to speak to the bus. *There is no harm in trying after all*, she thought.

'Hello,' Beatrice said in a tiny, timid voice. She felt both strangely hopeful and silly at the same time. Imagine Beatrice's reaction when the bus blinked and replied,

'Oh! Hello!'

Beatrice stood there, dumbstruck. There was a loud noise. *Thump-Thump*. It was her heart, hammering in her chest fast and hard. But WAIT! If she wasn't a wizard, was all this real or was she just dreaming it?

'Can you ... can you really talk, Mr Bus?' she said, just to be sure.

'Of course I can. Does that seem strange to you?' the bus replied grouchily.

'Oh no! Not at all — I mean, not completely,' she said, trying to reassure herself and *him* that talking to a red London Bus was the most natural thing in the world. 'And ... you ... snore too?'

'Me? No, since when do I snore?' the bus harrumphed.

'You ... you were snoring just now.'

'Um ... I was taking a nap. I don't snore,' replied the London Bus feeling embarrassed, his pride a bit bruised. 'But it doesn't surprise me that you're surprised that I can talk. Most humans can't hear me talking because they don't believe I can talk. That's exactly why I don't talk to them.' The bus was speaking in a very serious voice as if he was explaining something of great importance. 'But you must be quite special if you can hear me,' he continued, looking at the girl with more interest.

'Me? No sir ... Mr Bus, I am not that special,' she replied timidly, still feeling confused.

'I am pretty sure you are.'

'Thank you, Mr Bus.' Dreaming about a talking London bus was one thing, but talking to a real London Bus felt a little bit strange, although truly wonderful.

'Don't you ever talk to your passengers?' Beatrice asked, her mind clogged up with a thousand questions.

'*Especially* not to my passengers. They can be very rude, you see. I never talk to them ... unless the passenger is very special,' the London Bus explained, sounding less grumpy.

'Sir ... Mr Bus, may I ask you ... another question?' she said timidly.

'Speak now or forever hold your peace, child,' the Bus declared in a pompous voice.

'OK, I'll speak now. Where's your driver?'

'I don't have a driver. I don't need one. I drive myself.'

'That's exactly what I told my mum, but

she didn't believe me.'

'Oh, I am not surprised, my dear. Human grown-ups can be a bit messed up in the head at times ... erm confused. It's never easy with them.'

'I agree but Sir ... Mr Bus, may I ask you another question?'

'Speak now or forever hold your peace, child.'

'OK, I'll speak now. Did you hear my song the other night?'

'Which song? Did you sing a song?'

'I ... I ... did,' Beatrice replied, befuddled. *He didn't hear me singing? So my magic-spell song didn't actually have anything to do with this talking London Bus?* she wondered. It all sounded very puzzling — a mystery for sure.

'What's your name, child?' the London Bus asked.

'My name is Beatrice. But my mum and my classmates call me Bea. I don't like that — I like to be called by my full name ... Beatrice.'

'OK then, I will call you by your full name,' the London Bus replied.

Even though the Bus had a grumpy look stamped on his metal glazed face, Beatrice thought he was great fun.

'What's your name ... sir ... Mr Bus?' she asked.

'168 via Waterloo,' he announced proudly,

bending his flat metal roofed head to show his destination board. '168 is my name, via Waterloo my surname.' There was a long silence, then Beatrice heard a noise. *Thump-Thump-Thump*. It was her heart again, beating faster and harder.

'You? You ... are ... number 168?' she asked as she stared at the Bus with big wide eyes.

'Mind you!' he blurted out, 'I don't like to be called number 168. Passengers do it all the time and I find it terribly irritating. *I have to catch number 168. Where's number 168? Number 168 is late, number 168 is never on time!*' he growled, imitating the voices and the annoyed faces of some of the rudest passengers.

'I like to be called by my name and surname — 168 via Waterloo, always,' he said firmly.

'I am so sorry, I'll never do that again. So, you really are the 168 via Waterloo? The last Routemaster in the world, who's only friends with the brave and the bold? Is that really you?' Beatrice asked incredulously.

'If it looks like a duck, swims like a duck and quacks like a duck, then it probably is a duck — I am indeed not a duck, but the last Routemaster Bus in London and in the world!' he said, chortling at his own joke.

Beatrice was spellbound.

'I ... I ... I ... have a model bus at home. It has the same number — I mean, same name and surname as you ... and it's a Routemaster Bus too,' she explained.

'Well, I am not surprised,' remarked the Bus, looking pleased with himself, 'they've made a model that looks just like me, and gave my name 168 and — of course — my surname, via Waterloo, to it. That Bus is me. You see, I am famous.'

Things were getting even more confusing now for our poor Beatrice. *OK, the bus didn't hear me singing, but I think it was really my magic-spell song that turned my model bus into this real talking London Bus,* she thought. *The Bus said that the model bus is him!*

'You said you're famous?'

'That's right.'

'Everyone in my class wants to be famous. What are you famous for, 168 via Waterloo?'

'Some time ago, a very special passenger used to catch the 168 via Waterloo — ME, precisely,' explained the London Bus, clearing his piped throat. 'He travelled with me from one side of the city to the other and always got off at the same spot before going back home. We also used to meet up every Sunday, which is my day off, and we travelled together without the rude passengers.'

'Wow!'

'Precisely. Wow! We spent many wonderful days together and had the greatest fun in the world. He made my day, every day — he was the apple of my eye,' the Bus sighed, a nostalgic expression upon his metal glazed face.

'Why was this passenger so special?' asked Beatrice.

'Because ... he made me feel very special — everyone likes to feel special, Beatrice. He was ginger coloured and very funny. He was a cat, my dear — a beautiful ginger cat called Pepe.'

'A ginger cat?'

'That's right. Then one day a journalist saw Pepe travelling with me during my rides across London,' continued the Bus, 'and he thought that our friendship was an incredible story for his newspaper. I said, *"No! We don't want to be in the papers, leave us alone!"* He couldn't hear me, of course — only special people can ... and some less special,' the Bus added, clearing his piped throat again.

'But the journalist took a picture of us, wrote an article and bingo! We became famous overnight. We couldn't believe it! Every journalist in London wanted to take pictures of us and write articles about us, Pepe really enjoyed all the attention.'

'Oh that's such a stratospheric, super *mega-galactic* story!' Beatrice gushed.

'Precisely. Incredibly ... um ... stratospheric.'

'But what exactly is a *journa-litter*, 168 via Waterloo?'

Beatrice was always eager to learn new words. But her imagination was so big that whenever she repeated them, more often than not she'd get tangled up or she'd simply come up with entirely different words.

'A journalist, you mean?'

'That's it!'

'It's not a thing — well not a thing to eat at least,' the Bus replied, laughing again at his own joke. 'It's a person who writes stories for a living.'

'Real stories or make-believe?'

'Well, it depends. Sometimes these stories are real, sometimes just fibs ... um ... you know ... a load of balderdash and piffle. Journalists write stories for newspapers, radio and TV.'

'TV?' Lots of kids in my class want to be on TV,' said Beatrice, 'But they haven't done anything important. I mean, not like  you and the ginger cat. You should be very happy.'

'My dear, I am not exactly a spring chicken you see, and I am a bit behind the times. A real Routemaster Bus doesn't really care about being famous,' the bus explained, trying to show that he didn't make a big fuss about being well-known.

'It's certainly not fun when a bunch of annoying journalists interrupt your well-deserved daily nap between rides to take pictures of you, but Pepe liked that very much. So, that's how Pepe and I became famous, and that's why there is a model bus named after me.'

But 168 via Waterloo wasn't just famous, he was quite unique — very different from both the new funky double-decker buses that were travelling around London and the other old double-decker buses. *He* was a Routemaster Bus, a very old and traditional London bus — the first Routemaster Bus built in London and the last one that was still allowed to drive around. All the others Routemaster buses had been sent to the scrapheap. The 168 via Waterloo had large twinkling, glazed eyes and a big metallic mouth, which only special people could see, and of course, no human driver to be seen. Something that somehow, human passengers didn't notice. He was also known in town as *Grumpy*. Needless to say, he disliked that nickname very much.

The Routemaster Bus was also the old red bus beloved by Londoners past and present, by tourists from near and far and by the Queen of England herself who once said, ... *as the very last Routemaster Bus in London and in the world, the 168 via Waterloo is the symbol of the most English Englishness of all England, its surroundings and its map.*

The 168 via Waterloo was incredibly chuffed to hear that but, even though he was English through and through from his front mounted engine-heart to each red fibre of his metallic being, he had a secret passion for Italian desserts. His favourite was a dessert called Tiramisu.

At night, the Bus parked himself inside the London Transport Museum — known in town as Trotter. Here the most ancient buses, trains and cabs of the United Kingdom had retired after many years of serving London's passengers and were now happily enjoying the attention of tourists from near and far. To be fair, 168 via Waterloo didn't park exactly inside the museum but right outside the main entrance because — unlike all the other very ancient buses — he was terribly afraid of driving indoors.

Despite the fact that he was an old London Bus, 168 via Waterloo was the youngest of the group; 'the baby of the gang' as the London Transport Museum — a very kind, knowledgeable and well-spoken museum — affectionately called him. 168 via Waterloo

168 VIA WATERLOO'S HOME

was also the only old vehicle that was still allowed to leave the building every morning. The Bus considered the London Transport Museum his home.

The old Bus and Beatrice were still chatting to each other when, suddenly they heard a loud squeaking voice from further away.

'Beaaaaaaa!'

'Oh no! The *dream-flusher!* I must go!' said Beatrice, grimacing.

'The *dream-flusher?* What is that?' asked the London Bus.

'My mum! I forgot about her! But ... 168 via

Waterloo, before I go, may I ask you another question?'

'Speak now or forever hold your peace, child.'

'OK, I'll speak now.' Beatrice took a deep breath and said, 'What if everything sucks? I mean, what are you supposed to do?'

'Er, *sucks*? Harrumph.' The London Bus cleared his piped throat, feeling embarrassed. He was not accustomed to using such a word.

'Well ... I guess everyone must figure out such things for themselves. A lot of things ... er ... suck, I agree with you but I'm not sure that "everything" sucks — harrumph. Why do you think this way?'

'Because at home I am bored, and at school I am super-bored. I'd like to travel, visit new places and see new things. And what I would really like to do is hang out with a London Bus. A Routemaster Bus, precisely! A Bus like you,' said Beatrice smiling. 'Am I really nuts?'

'Oh bless you. You're just like my old friend Pepe! Thank you, Beatrice,' the London Bus replied, swelling with pride. He was very pleased to hear that she considered him fun to be with.

'I knew you'd understand!' cried Beatrice. 'It was super nice to meet you 168 via Waterloo!' Beatrice didn't want to go.

'Well, it was ... super nice to meet you too, young lady,' the Bus answered politely, bowing his flat roofed head while making sure his hat didn't fall off. Every sign of his previous grumpiness had now disappeared from his glazed window face. The London Bus was happy that a human — even if only a little one — had taken the time to talk to him. *She must be a very brave and bold girl,* he thought.

'168 via Waterloo ... can I meet you again?' Beatrice asked tentatively.

'If you wish, you will. And remember, I can talk, but only very special people can hear me. There aren't many of us talking buses left in London, just like there aren't many special people around who can hear me. You're one of them. Goodbye now my dear and see you around!'

'Goodbye now and see you around!' replied Beatrice, enchanted. She gave him her best smile and dashed off.

'I knew it! I knew he could talk, I just knew it!' she muttered under her breath.

On the drive home, Beatrice pinched her arm very hard, just to make sure that she wasn't dreaming.

'Ow!' she squealed. No, she wasn't — it had all been incredibly real. Dream number 2, *the missing dream,* had just come true after singing her magic song, somehow.

The 168 via Waterloo model bus was now as big as the other regular buses in the street.

Beatrice didn't care much how all that had happened — the London Bus was real and he had talked to her. But would she get to see him again, and maybe even go on a ride around London with him?

When Beatrice arrived home, she went straight to her bedroom to fetch her model bus but strangely, it was not there.

'Where is it?' she said out loud to the room.

She searched everywhere — under the bed, in her wardrobe and in every single drawer.

'My bus!' she gasped.

Chapter Five

LOOSING
HOPE

'Where is it, Mum?'

'Where is what, dear?'

'My Routemaster bus! It's gone!'

'I don't know, darling — ask your dad. Or
maybe, it just drove off,' her mum replied,
teasing her.

'Mum, that's not funny!' Beatrice rushed to her dad's studio. As usual, Mr Goodenough was reading his newspaper.

'Have you seen it, Dad?'

'What, darling?'

'My bus! It's gone!'

'No my dear, ask your brother, he might have taken it by mistake.'

'Andrew!' Beatrice shouted, banging her fists as hard as she could against the locked door of her brother's bedroom.

'What do you want?' Andrew grunted.

'My Routemaster bus! Where did you put my bus, Andrew?'

But no further reply came from the bedroom. Andrew had put on his headphones and was now busy playing one of his favourite video games — *The Warrior with Six Fingers and Eight Feet*.

'Andrew!' Beatrice screamed louder — tears streaming down her face like rain gushing off a steep roof.

'I guess he means no,' said Mr Goodenough as he went to check on his daughter. 'You know that he's not interested in your things — he's obsessed with his video games.'

Beatrice looked at her dad in dismay and marched to her bedroom. She opened the wardrobe, jumped in, snuggled up and fell asleep.

The day after at school, all Beatrice could think about was the mysterious appearance of the talking bus and the unexplainable disappearance of her model bus.

But hang on! My model bus has gone because I tried to turn it into a big talking bus with my magic spell-song, and that's exactly why I don't have it anymore, she thought. *That means that my magic song worked. How come I didn't think of that!* she reasoned. *I have to speak to Mark!*

At break time Beatrice went straight to Mark's classroom.

'Mark, you won't believe this!'

'*W-w-what*?'

'The most awful and the most amazing thing has happened to me!'

'What has *h-h-happened* to you?'

'Do you remember the red bus you gave me?'

'Yes.'

'It's disappeared! That's the awful thing.'

'That's *a-a-awful!* Did your *b-b-brother* take it?'

'No Mark, the model bus has turned into a real bus, that's why I don't have it anymore!'

'That *c-c-can't* be possible.'

'I know it can't be but it is! OK, do you remember dream number two?'

'*N-n-no.* You didn't have dream number two

— it was *m-m-missing*. I *r-r-remember* dream number three about the very *b-b-best* friend *f-f-forever*, which came true *b-b-because* you met *m-m-me*.'

'Oh, I came up with dream number two! It was about my wish to turn the bus that you gave to me into a real bus. Do you remember I told you that I came up with a magic song to make that happen?'

'Yes, *d-d-did* it work?' he stuttered.

'That's what I am saying. It did! I mean, I think it did. The bus isn't at home anymore! It's in the street now and it's huge. It must have worked. I have turned the model bus into a real bus! What do you think?'

'I don't know. I don't *u-u-understand*.'

'Oh Mark, it's simple! The 168 via Waterloo is no longer a model bus, but it's as big as the big buses in the streets of London and guess what?'

'*W-w-what?*'

'He talks! And that's the amazing thing!'

'You're just telling *f-f-fibs*, Beatrice!' he retorted, trying to sound smart.

'I don't tell fibs, Mark! It's true. I met him the other day, but the Bus said that most people can't hear him talking. Only special people can.'

'A *t-t-talking* Bus?'

'Yes. A talking Bus.'

'But if you *c-c-can* hear him talking, does that *m-m-mean* you're special?'

'That's what the Bus said. I mean, I've told him that I am not that special but he insisted,' Beatrice continued. 'Mark, please don't tell this to anyone, OK? If my classmates find out that I now even talk to buses, they'll think I am completely nuts and they'll tease me forever and ever!'

'OK, OK I won't, but *a-a-are* you *s-s-sure* that it was your *m-m-magic* song that made it happen?'

'I think so.'

'But if it was your magic *s-s-s-song*, then you're a *w-w-wizard?*'

'No, Mark, wizards don't exist. I mean, not in London at least. Anyone can do a magic spell from time to time — you don't need to be a wizard for that. I think. Well, actually I am not completely sure it was my magic song because the talking 168 via Waterloo said that he has never heard me singing.'

'That's quite *s-s-strange*. What else did he say?'

'Many things, Mark.'

Beatrice started telling him the entire story of the 168 via Waterloo, about his friend Pepe — the missing ginger cat — and about how the two had become famous.

'Wow! That's a wicked *s-s-story*,' gushed

Mark.

'Yes, really wicked! I must go now, break time is almost over! See you soon.'

'See you *s-s-soon*, Beatrice,' replied Mark, gazing at her in awe. He could not believe his friend's incredible good luck.

That same day, Beatrice couldn't wait for her mum to pick her up from school.

'Mum, can we please stop by Caramba Café?' Beatrice asked on their way home. 'I'd like an ice cream.'

'There's ice cream at home and you have too much homework to do,' snapped her mother.

'But I like that ice cream. Can we at least drive by, please?' she insisted. Beatrice didn't want to tell her mum that she was looking for a talking Routemaster Bus — her mum would have thought she had gone mad.

'OK, but we won't stop. Not today.'

'All right, Mum. Thanks.'

As the car approached the Caramba Café, Beatrice looked outside the window, eager to find the Bus. To her great disappointment, the place where 168 via Waterloo was parked last time was now empty. She leaned back in her seat feeling disappointed.

'Where is he?' she muttered under her breath, frowning. Over the following days, Beatrice asked her mother to drive past the café again, but somehow, the mysterious

London Bus was never there. Could it possibly be that the bus was just doing his daily rides across the city? Most probably, but then again, the Bus was not there the day after, the day after that and the day after that.

'Why do you like this route so much?' asked Mrs Goodenough.

Beatrice didn't answer — tears ran down her round rosy cheeks. She immediately wiped them away because she did not want her mum to see that she was crying.

Where is the talking Bus? Was it all just a dream then? Was the story written by the journalitter ... just a fib? After all, the Bus had said that jour ... journal ... journalists are mostly telling fibs! she thought. All these questions filled Beatrice's mind. *No! It was all real*, she concluded.

'Grown-ups lie at times and can be a bit messed up in the head or confused as 168 via Waterloo said, but not a Routemaster Bus! I am sure of that,' she said to herself. It was time to search for her new-but-already-lost friend.

Chapter Six

IN SEARCH OF 168 VIA WATERLOO

The next day at school, Beatrice asked Miss Pauline to help her. Miss Pauline, Beatrice's favourite teacher, was half-English and half-French. She had shoulder length blonde hair, almond-shaped blue eyes and a beautiful, gentle smile.

'Miss Pauline, I am looking for a piece of paper in a *passpepper* written by a *journalitter* who has written a story about a ginger cat travelling on a London bus. Can you help me find this piece of paper?' she asked eagerly.

'Do you mean an article in a newspaper written by a journalist?' the teacher replied with a smile.

'That's it!'

'And why are you looking for this article?'

'Because I want to find the cat, I've heard he became very famous because he was travelling on this bus and I'd like to have my picture taken with him.'

'And ... with the bus. Is that right?' asked Miss Pauline who knew about Beatrice's love for buses.

'Um ... yes, that's right. And with the bus.'

Beatrice liked Miss Pauline very much, however she didn't think it was too wise to tell her that she had met a talking bus, which most probably was her model bus.

Andrew already said that she was as annoying as an ugly fly — she didn't want Miss Pauline to think that she was as crazy as a buzzing bee.

'Meet me tomorrow at the school library at noon. We'll find what you're looking for,' promised Miss Pauline.

'Great! Thank you Miss! See you tomorrow!'

The next day in the library, sitting in front of an old computer, Beatrice and Miss Pauline were searching for clues.

'So Beatrice, do you know when this article was published?' Miss Pauline asked.

'I don't, Miss,' replied Beatrice, 'but the name of the ginger cat is Pepe and the name of the London Bus—' she hesitated, 'I mean, the number of the bus is 168 and it goes via Waterloo. And the story is real,' she added, just to be clear. Miss Pauline started typing fast on the keyboard and soon hundreds of images of the 168 via Waterloo and the ginger cat called Pepe came up on the screen, followed by numerous articles.

'Of course! This is the 168 via Waterloo, I remember now! *The very last Routemaster in the world, who's only friends with the brave and the bold.* And Pepe,' said Miss Pauline, smiling.

'Do you know *him?* I mean ... *it?*' asked Beatrice, correcting herself.

'Of course I do, everyone does. These two are very famous. The number of articles that have been written about them would make the Queen green with envy!'

Does Miss Pauline know that this London Bus can talk? Beatrice wondered.

'The cat looks quite vain. He seems to enjoy the limelight,' said Miss Pauline, sounding amused.

'*Lemon* ...? What does *lemonlight* mean?'

'Limelight, dear. Enjoying the limelight means that a lot of people pay attention to you and you like it.'

'Does that mean they love you?'

'Just because people pay attention to you, it doesn't necessarily mean they love you.'

'My Mum doesn't pay much attention to me and I am not sure she loves me.'

'I'm sure she does,' replied Miss Pauline with a reassuring smile as she enlarged one of the images on the computer screen.

'Here's the article from the *Daily Fairy Tales* newspaper about the ginger cat and the Routemaster Bus you're talking about.'

'Great! Does it say where the cat is?' asked Beatrice eagerly.

'The owner of the cat is a chef who has a restaurant,' added Miss Pauline. 'His name is Mr Cecco. He's Italian. You should ask your mum to take you there for lunch or dinner sometime. The article says that his specialty is pasta and Tiramisu, a delicious Italian dessert.'

'And where is Mr Cecco's restaurant, Miss?' Not waiting for an answer, Beatrice leaned forward to read the article herself.

'It's close to school. The address is 32 Puppet Street,' replied Miss Pauline.

'Thank you, Miss,' said Beatrice. And she skipped off home.

Chapter Seven

A WEB OF LIES

Beatrice wondered how she could find Puppet Street and Mr Cecco's restaurant. *A map! I need a map, the right map*, she thought.

Beatrice hoped that once she had found the cat, he would tell her where to find her new-but-already-lost friend, the very famous 168 via Waterloo. *After all, if the cat is the London Bus' best friend, and the Bus is a talking bus, surely Pepe is a talking cat*, she thought.

'There must be something in here,' she murmured as she was searching through the shelves of the bookcase in the lounge when she spotted a big book called the *Maps of the World.*

'There it is!' she sighed in relief. Beatrice stood on her toes and stretched out one arm to grab the large and heavy book but it was too far out of reach. She dragged a little stool up to the bookcase and climbed up on it.

'Oh no! I can't get it! It's still too far,' she exclaimed when suddenly, the book fell off the shelf and landed on the floor. It almost hit Beatrice on her very round head.

'*Holly crisps*! How did that happen? I didn't even touch it,' she cried.

The book contained lots of maps — the map of North America, the map of South America, the map of Europe, the map of Asia, the map of Africa, the map of Australia, the map of Antarctica and, of course, the map of United Kingdom.

Beatrice jumped off the stool, picked up the book and began rifling through the pages when another very mysterious thing happened — all the maps started flying out of the book. They were now frantically bobbing up and down right in front of her nose. Beatrice felt dizzy. She squinted her eyes, wrinkled her nose and scratched its tip.

Since she had sung that magic-spell song to the model bus, weird and strange things had started to happen around her, even though she wasn't a wizard and had never wished to be one. But that was not all — a voice coming out of one of the maps said,

'Beatrice, do you know where your school is?'

'A speaking map?' Beatrice said flinching and feeling bewildered. *And how does she know my name?* she wondered.

'Indeed, I am a speaking Map. So do you know where your school is, Beatrice?' the Map insisted.

'Yes I ... I do it's ... it's in London.'

'Good, you must use me then because London is in Asia — in China, precisely. I am the Map of Asia, nice to meet you, Beatrice,' said the Map of Asia. Right then another Map broke into the conversation roaring with laughter.

'Ha-ha-ha-ha.' It was the Map of Africa. 'Child, don't listen to her. The Map of Asia is a big show-off. London is in the Map of Africa! Check me instead!' said the Map of Africa, jumping close to Beatrice's face, so closely that she had to gently push her away with her palm.

'Stop it at once you two,' shouted a third Map loudly.

'Who are you?' Beatrice asked curiously.

'I am the Map of Europe,' replied the third Map. 'Beatrice, don't listen to those attention seekers! London is in Europe. In France, precisely,' explained the Map of Europe, feeling self-important.

All of a sudden, another Map hurried over to Beatrice — she had a horrified expression on her map-face and was looking utterly flustered.

'They are talking complete nonsense! That's an unlawful appropriation of something that belongs to me!' the Map shrieked, glaring at the other Maps reproachfully. 'To me and only to me! Have I made myself clear?'

But the other Maps didn't seem too bothered — some of them sighed, shaking their map-heads, others rolled their map-eyes and all of them were ignoring the tense and agitated Map.

'Besides, this is the most terrible lie I have ever heard,' the Map kept complaining, trying at the same time to regain her composure.

Looking at Beatrice, she then said,

'My sweet child, please do not let yourself be fooled by those squabbling Maps. London is not exactly in the Map of Europe, or maybe it is — who knows ! But it's certainly not in France!'

'Who are you?' asked Beatrice, still feeling dizzy and so unable to read the name of the Map.

'I'm the Map of the United Kingdom. How do you do?' the Map said politely, now smiling and curtsying at the same time.

'Oh I am sorry! I should have recognised you!' replied Beatrice. 'Hello!'

'That's OK,' she said, sighing. 'The Map of the United Kingdom includes the Map of England, the Map of Wales, the Map of Scotland and the Map of Northern Ireland. London is in the Map of England. Trust me,' continued the Map, speaking in a pompous manner.

'Yes, I know,' said Beatrice, 'Miss Pauline told us in class that London is in the Map of England, and that's why I am English, but why are all the other Maps lying?'

'Well, they are not lying exactly. They just think London is a very great city and they like to believe it's theirs,' she said in a more friendly and reassuring way.

'Really?'

'Really. It might look as if it's a web of lies, but to be honest with you, I think they are just quite bad at geography. Every time it's the same story and I have to remind them where London really is!' Meanwhile, all the other Maps had stopped bickering and began dancing in a circle.

Floating around the room and holding hands tightly, they were now telling each other jokes and laughing loudly.

It was quite a scene — Beatrice had never seen anything like it before.

'Oh! That's so super *galactically* cool! You should all come to visit me at school during our geography class sometime — I am sure

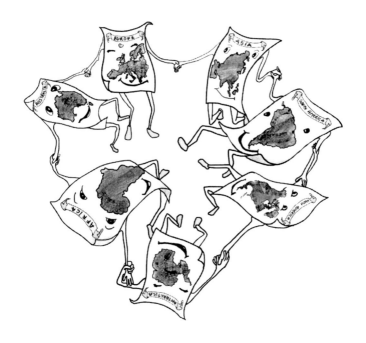

Miss Pauline would like it! She's a really fun teacher.'

'Well, my child, I can't speak for the other Maps but I will certainly pay a visit.'

'Great! But, Map of the United Kingdom, who's that big Map up there?'

A rather large Map had separated from the group and was flying towards the ceiling, but so fast that she crashed against it. From up there, she looked down on the other Maps who were now gently floating towards the floor.

'That's the Map of North America. She always does that. She has a mind of her own. That's the way she is!.'

'North America?'

'Yes, my dear. The Map of North America includes two large countries, the United States and Canada. She's the only Map who doesn't bother to say that London belongs to her,' explained the Map of the United Kingdom.

'Why? Is she really good at geography?'

'Not exactly, none of us really are, in truth. It's just that the Map of Canada has her very own city called London, a tiny city but a London all the same. The Map of the United States, instead, has a great city of her own called New York — she always says that her city is so great that she doesn't need London,' said the Map in a serious voice.

But despite all those explanations, Beatrice was getting more and more confused. She squinted her eyes, wrinkled her nose and scratched its tip, trying to decide what to do next. She wasn't quite sure whether she should trust any of those Maps — they all seemed quite nuts after all.

I'd better double-check with Dad, she thought and went to see him in his study.

As usual, Mr Goodenough was reading his favourite newspaper.

'Dad, is London in the Map of England and is the Map of England part of the Map of the United Kingdom?' she asked.

'Precisely,' her dad answered, his nose stuck in his newspaper.

'Are you sure?'

'I am sure.'

'Cool, thanks Dad!' Beatrice dashed back to the lounge.

'There you are,' said the Map of the United Kingdom as Beatrice returned, 'So are you going to pick me?'

'Yes. I am, but are you ready?'

'Ready for what?' the Map answered with a confused expression on her map-face.

'For my big mission!'

'Of course I am, I love big missions!' gushed the Map. 'But hang on, what sort of mission exactly, if you don't mind me asking. You see, I am only a Map and I don't really want to get into too much trouble.'

'Oh no trouble at all Ms Map, don't worry! I just need to find Puppet Street in London — Mr Cecco's restaurant is there. I am looking for his ginger cat Pepe.'

'I see, well, that's easy then — allow me to help you, my dear. I am a Map after all!' replied the Map of the United Kingdom, giggling. 'And now, watch me go!' The Map took a deep breath and announced grandly,

'Ladies and gentlemen ... TA-DA ... right in front of your eyes, you can admire the spectacular, amazing, wonderful ... the super fantastic Map of London!'

Leaving a trail of glittering, golden powder, the Map of the United Kingdom spun as fast as a washing machine spinner and turned into nothing less than the Map of the most famous city in the United Kingdom:

LONDON

'Oh! Are you some kind of wizard?' gushed Beatrice.

'Who? Me? No dear, I am not. There are no wizards in London .. only magicians. And, I can gladly say that I am neither of the two — I just like to do some magic from time to time. We can all do it.'

'That's what I said to my BFF!'

'Your BFF? What on earth is a BFF?'

'My best friend forever!'

'Oh, I see, that's terribly sweet. We — Maps — do not have BFFs.'

'Why not?'

'We can't — we change our map-minds all the time,' replied the Map, chuckling.

Meanwhile, spellbound by the amazing performance the Map of the United Kingdom had put on, all the other Maps

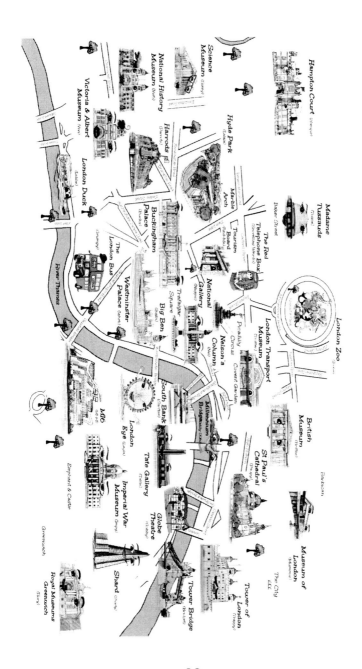

Hampton Court (Uxbridge)

Science Museum (Surrey)

National History Museum (Kent)

Victoria & Albert Museum (West)

Hyde Park (Ladies)

Harrods (Herrick)

London Duck (Ladies)

Marble Arch

Baker Street

Madame Tussauds (Greene)

The Red Telephone Box (Streatline Wards)

Tourism Board (Fenchley)

Buckingham Palace (Bucks)

The London Bus (Grumpy)

Westminster Palace (West)

National Gallery (Staples)

Big Ben (East)

Trafalgar Square

Picadilly Circus

Nelson's Column (Out)

Covent Garden

London Transport Museum (Surrey)

London Zoo (Lions)

British Museum (Forties)

St Paul's Cathedral (Preky)

Museum of London (Putney) The City LLL

Tower of London (Troops)

Museum of London (Autumns)

Blackburn

South Bank (Surrey)

Millenium Bridge (Beds)

London Eye (Lions)

Tate Gallery (Notts)

Imperial War Museum (Grey)

Globe Theatre (Derby)

Shard (Chess)

Tower Bridge (Benfield)

MI6 (068x8)

Elephant & Castle

Greenwich

Royal Museums Greenwich (Bury)

River Thames

started clapping enthusiastically, showing heir friendlier side to the *Map-of-the-United-Kingdom-turned-Map-of-London*.

Though truthfully, they were a bit jealous that they had not been able to do this magic trick themselves.

Then, slowly and gently, all the Maps began dancing their way back into the book. All of them apart from the Map of North America who was still floating in the air, refusing to follow the other Maps into the *Maps of the World* book.

Beatrice picked up the *Map-of-United Kingdom-turned-Map-of-London*, gently laid her down on the floor and begun searching for the name of the street. After a good while, she found what she was looking for.

'There it is, Puppet Street!' she gushed.

'Good girl, you know how to use me then!' exclaimed Map.

Beatrice smiled, took a red pencil and drew a big circle around Puppet Street.

'Hey! Don't push that pointy thing too hard! You're hurting me!' the Map cried in pain.

'Oh, I am sorry!'

Beatrice took the Map and went to ring her BFF.

'Mark! Mark! Come on, pick up!'

'*H-h-hello*,' Mark replied on the other end of the phone.

'Mark, listen to this. I have not only met a talking Bus but also talking Maps!'

'*W-w-when?* Where?'

'Just now! At home!'

'That's *r-r-rubbish!* I don't *b-b-believe* you, *B-B-Beatrice*. You're *m-m-making* things up, and you're *t-t-trying* to make a *m-m-monkey* out of me!' protested Mark.

But GUESS WHAT? The Map heard Mark. Needless to say, she felt terribly offended.

'What? Rubbish? We are made of PAPER not rubbish! Your BFF is rude, Beatrice! You must change him. At once!' the Map of London said in a commanding voice.

'Quiet, please! I can't change him,' Beatrice whispered to the Map.

'Why not?' the Map insisted.

'Because he's my BFF and BFFs are forever not for a short while!'

'Oh, I see. That's terribly sweet.'

'Beatrice, whom are you *s-s-speaking* to?' Mark asked, alarmed.

'Mark, I am speaking to the Map of London. I told you, Maps can talk! She's here with me — she heard you and she got offended. She thought you called her rubbish. And no, I am not making things up. You're my BFF, why would I lie to you?'

'I don't *k-k-know*. To be *c-c-cool?*'

'Mark, I am cool even if my classmates at

school think I am a bit weird. I mean, the Bus thinks I am cool anyway.'

'And what did these Maps say to you?' Mark asked suspiciously.

'Oh, just fibs really! They were all lying. All the Maps said that London belonged to them. The only one who wasn't lying was the Map of the United Kingdom who has turned into the Map of London. Well, I hope she wasn't lying!' Beatrice said, lowering her voice as she didn't want her new *map-friend* to hear her.

'I don't think she *d-d-did*. London *r-r-really* belongs to the Map of the United Kingdom. I *m-m-mean*, we live in the United Kingdom, *d-d-don't* we?' asked Mark.

'Yes, we do,' replied Beatrice.

But the *Map-of-the-United-Kingdom-turned-Map-of-London* overheard them again, and again she expressed all her disappointment.

'No, no, no! That's no good! I've heard you Beatrice. I don't lie — you should trust me by now!'

'OK! I trust you but please stay quiet for a moment Map of London! I am talking to my BFF,' Beatrice whispered.

'All right, all right, I will shut my mouth!' the Map whispered back.

'Are you still *t-t-talking* to the Map?'

'Sorry, Mark. I am.'

'OK *b-b-but* ... why, Beatrice?'

'Why what, Mark?

'Why is this not *h-h-happening* to me too?'

'What's not happening to you?'

'That *t-t-things* talk to me like they *t-t-talk* to you? I *m-m-mean*, it would be fun if one of my *t-t-trucks* talked to me, or my water gun.'

'I don't know Mark — try to come up with a magic song, like I did.'

'OK, I am going to *t-t-try*. Bye Beatrice!'

'Bye Mark!'

Beatrice gently folded the Map of London and put her in her pink school bag. She was ready to find her *new-but-already-lost-friend*, the famous 168 via Waterloo — the talking London Bus. It would be an adventure!

A mission! Certainly, A BIG MISSION!

Chapter Eight

A BIG
MISSION

'**M**um, can I walk back home by myself today after school? A lot my classmates do it already,' Beatrice asked the next morning as Mrs Goodenough drove her to school.

Beatrice lived about twenty minutes away

by foot from Bell-Bell School. The streets in the area where she lived were swarming with parents and kids and were very safe.

'All right, it's about time you grew up a bit — you're eight years old now. But don't talk to strangers and be careful. Maybe you could ask your little friend ... what's his name ... to walk with you.'

'Nine, Mum,' Beatrice corrected her. 'OK, I won't talk to strangers. And his name is Mark, Mum.'

'Of course, darling. Nine ... Mark ... yes Mark.'

Her mum was right, it was about time she grew up a bit, Beatrice thought. But not too much because she didn't want to turn into one of those weird, complicated grown-ups who have lost all their imagination.

After school, humming her little magic spell song and holding the Map of London in front of her with both hands, Beatrice made her way to Puppet Street. When she reached a roundabout, she stopped to take a closer look at her Map friend.

'Beatrice, don't bother to check *me* for directions. My sixth sense is telling me that you need to turn left and then left again,' explained the Map.

'Sixth sense? What's that?'

'My intuition, my gut feeling, guessing!

Whatever you want to call it.'

'OK, but in here it says — I mean, YOU say that I have to turn right and right again,' insisted Beatrice. Holding the Map with one hand, she slid one finger over the red circle, which made the Map burst into hysterical laughter.

'Beatrice stop! You're tickling me!'

'Oh, I am sorry!'

'OK, let me explain Beatrice. We — printed Maps — can make mistakes at times. As I said, we're not necessarily good at geography — actually, quite often we don't have a clue about it. The problem is that once we have been printed, if something changes in that city or in that country, we can get a bit out of date.'

'You're an out-of-date Map?'

'Well yes, that's how I feel, completely out of date. And when it's like that, then you just have to follow your instincts. And my instincts are now telling me that you have to turn left and left again. There you will find Puppet Street. Trust me.'

'All right, I will do as you say!' Following the Map of London's instructions, Beatrice turned left and left again and spotted a big road sign, which read: 'Puppet Street'.

'There it is! she gushed. The Map of London was right — Puppet Street was exactly where she said it would be.

'Well, my mission has been accomplished, I guess,' announced the chatty Map.

'And mine is just starting now! Thanks Map of London!'

'Obliged! Good luck girl!' The Map flew off and vanished in a split second, leaving a shimmering trail behind. Beatrice stood in awe for a bit then she looked at the other side of the road and spotted another sign, which read, 'Mr Cecco's Restaurant'

A large man came out of the restaurant. He was wearing a white apron, with the name 'Mr Cecco' stitched on it. He was standing outside looking for clients, since there were only a few inside. He had a big red face, thick brown hair and a moustache so long that two curls were hanging down from the corners of his mouth. He looked very jolly indeed.

'Are you Mr Cecco?' asked Beatrice as she approached him.

'I am indeed, young lady.'

'My name is Beatrice.'

'Hello Beatrice, what can I do for you?' answered the large man with a thick Italian accent. The Italian chef was very surprised to see such a young person looking for him.

'I am looking for a ginger cat called Pepe. My teacher told me he belongs to you.'

'Oh my poor Pepe, he's not here anymore.'

'Did you give him away?' Beatrice asked, sounding concerned.

'No, of course I didn't. But Pepe had a bit of a soft spot for London buses and the limelight,' Mr Cecco explained. 'He kept catching this London Bus — Routemaster 168 via Waterloo. He was travelling around London with this Bus every day when one day, a journalist wrote a story about the two of them and bingo! They both became very famous.'

Even though Beatrice knew the story already, she listened to him attentively.

'But Pepe wasn't like other cats,' said the big Italian man, 'he was very clever and a bit vain ... and one day, he disappeared.'

'He disappeared?'

'Exactly.'

'What about the Bus?'

'What about ... the Bus?' Mr Cecco echoed, looking at Beatrice with inquisitive eyes.

'Nothing, nothing.'

Although Mr Cecco was talking about Pepe as if he were a *talking* cat, Beatrice thought it was better not to tell him that 168 via Waterloo was a talking bus. *Or perhaps he knows too?* she wondered.

'I'm still looking for Pepe. Some people told me they've spotted him around town. I've been putting posters up everywhere. I hope I'll find him one day,'

said Mr Cecco, his face crumpling into a sad frown.

Beatrice felt deeply sorry for the old man. *He's lost his cat and I've lost my new friend the Routemaster Bus. We have a lot in common,* she thought. *And he's not that weird and complicated, for a grown-up.*

'And do you know where the 168 via Waterloo is now?' she asked, hesitantly.

'Oh, *he*'s where *he* always is. *He* stops in front of Caramba Café,' replied Mr Cecco referring to the bus as a *He* and not as an *It.*

'*He?*'

'Yes! *He*,' replied Mr Cecco, nodding and pushing his eyebrows very high.

Beatrice was flabbergasted.

Is Mr Cecco trying to tell me that he knows that 168 via Waterloo is a talking bus? If so, he must be one of those very special people in London who can hear him talking. Just like me, Beatrice thought.

'Mr Cecco, my mum drove me by the café the other day, and the day after and the day after that but I haven't seen ... *him*.'

'Oh but you'll only find *him* there in between rides,' explained the big man. 'You need to know when to go there. You need a timetable.'

'A *thumbletable?* What's a *thumbletable, Mr Cecco?*'

'A timetable,' he corrected her. 'A timetable

is a list that tells you when something is going to be somewhere.'

'Do you have one for me? A *thumb* ... I mean a ... timetable for the 168 via Waterloo?'

'Hang on, I think I do.' Mr Cecco put his hands in his big trousers pockets and started searching for something.

'There you go. Check this out,' he said handing the timetable to Beatrice. 'You remind me of my cat, so interested in this Bus.'

'But I'm not vain Mr Cecco and I'm not looking for the *lemonlight* like Pepe,' Beatrice giggled.

'The *lemonlight*? You mean, the limelight?'

'That's it!'

'Oh, that's good, my child. That's what most people want nowadays. Pepe liked the limelight but he was a very sweet and kind-hearted cat too. He also liked hats very much — his favourites were a driver's cap and a Mexican hat.'

'And does the 168 via Waterloo like the *lemon* ... limelight?' Beatrice asked pretending to joke around. She was trying to find out as much as possible about the Bus.

'Who knows. You'll have to ask *him*,' said Mr Cecco, winking and raising his eyebrows even higher and referring again to the Bus as a *He* rather than as an *It*.

Yes! Mr Cecco definitely knows, Beatrice thought.

'OK, I will ask ... *him*,' repeated Beatrice, looking at Mr Cecco inquisitively.

'You have a lot of imagination, young lady,' said the Italian chef.

'My Mum says that too! But she says that I have TOO much imagination and that makes me as annoying as a buzzing fly. My brother instead says that I am annoying as an ugly fly because I ask him way too many questions,' Beatrice explained, feeling less cheerful.

'Oh no, my dear, a lot of imagination is good — and TOO much imagination is even better. You see, if you want to be able to cook delicious dishes like pizza, pasta and Tiramisu, you need a lot of imagination. And to have a lot of imagination you need to believe in things other people don't see or that maybe, they just don't want to see. I call these things our DREAMS.'

'Oh, I know a lot about DREAMS, Mr Cecco! I have lots of dreams of my own but it's not easy when your mum is a *dream-flusher*.'

'A what?'

'A *dream-flusher!*' she repeated. 'She kills and flushes down ... er ... people's dreams, just like you would kill an annoying, buzzing and ugly fly.'

'Oh, I see!' Mr Cecco exclaimed, amused, 'Do you mean a dream-crusher?'

'That's it!'

'I am sorry to hear that, Beatrice but I would never hurt a fly, let alone kill one — even an *annoying, buzzing* or an ugly *fly*,' he replied.

'But hang on, before you go ...' Mr Cecco walked inside his restaurant and returned almost immediately with a lunch box in his hands.

'Take this. It's a Tiramisu, a special Italian dessert. My specialty,' he said. 'There are two portions here, one is for you and the other one is for you to give to someone you care about.' This time, he raised only his left eyebrow.

'Thank you, Mr Cecco! I will!' said Beatrice taking the lunch box from his hands.

I think Mr Cecco means that the Tiramisu is for the London Bus, but in case 168 via Waterloo doesn't like it, I will give it to Mark, she thought.

Suddenly, an annoying, ugly fly landed on Beatrice's nose.

'Get off you annoying, ugly fly!' she cried, disgusted.

Chapter Nine

GOOD OLD TIMES

The next day after school, armed with the timetable and a great determination to find her *new-but-already-lost* friend, Beatrice made her way to Caramba Café. She had worked out that she needed to be at the parking area, which was just by the Caramba

Café, by 3:15 pm. When she reached the Café, the big clock in the square showed 3:10 pm, but the 168 via Waterloo was nowhere to be seen.Beatrice sat on a bench in the little garden opposite to Caramba Café, her feet dangling in mid-air. She kept on checking the main road, the clock, the bus parking area and the timetable — her heart was racing fast — when finally a bus appeared in the distance.

'168 via Waterloo, 168 via Waterloo!' Beatrice screamed, jumping up and down and tingling with delight.

'Who is that?' asked the Routemaster Bus, squinting his old glazed eyes to see better as he reached the parking area. 'Oh, it's you, child. Where have you been? I haven't seen you in a while.'

'My mum has been driving me past almost every day but I couldn't find you!' Beatrice explained anxiously.

'Oh I am sorry,' replied the London Bus, 'I am so used to my daily rides that I forgot to tell you when you can find me in front of Caramba Café — but how did you know I was going to be here now?'

'I have a *thumb* ... a timetable. Mr Cecco gave it to me,' Beatrice replied.

'Mr Cecco?' the London Bus asked in a quizzing manner.

'Yes, Pepe's owner.'

'How do you know him?'

'It's a long story, 168 via Waterloo,' Beatrice said smiling. 'My teacher helped me find the piece of paper you told me was written by the *journalitter*.' Beatrice began to tell him the entire story.

'Yes, yes, the article, the journalist,' he corrected her, amused by Beatrice's words.

'I was looking for Pepe — I was hoping he'd tell me how to find you — so I went to Mr Cecco's restaurant but he told me that Pepe has disappeared. He doesn't know where he is any more.'

'I know, no one knows where Pepe is. It makes me so sad,' said 168 via Waterloo, a dark shadow crossed his metal-glazed-face.

'Do you miss him a lot?' asked Beatrice.

'I miss him a lot,' replied the Bus. 'He's the only best friend I have ever had.'

A couple of tears streamed down his metal-glazed face and splattered on the pavement producing a loud rattling noise.

'Every day I carry all these passengers around the city, but nobody ever says a kind word to me. I get really bored. Pepe used to be great company. As I said, he was a great cat. We used to have tea and Tiramisu that Mr Cecco made for us and tell each other funny stories about London. I have been looking for him everywhere,' the Bus said full of sorrow.

113

'I am sure he's around somewhere,' said Beatrice, trying to cheer him up. 'But .. does Mr Cecco know ... that you can talk?'

'Well, yes, he does ... he does, my dear. He's one of those special people in London with a big imagination who can hear me talking. That's exactly why he can hear me but please Beatrice, don't tell anyone that I can talk. If people can't figure it out for themselves, I don't want them to know. Don't let the cat out of the bag!'

'Oh, I won't, don't worry 168 via Waterloo!' Beatrice replied.

But WAIT! I have already told Mark, she

thought. *Well, Mark is my BFF and BFFs aren't just 'people',* she reasoned.

Suddenly, 168 via Waterloo noticed a long queue of nervous people standing at the bus stop.

'I am sorry, I need to get ready for my next ride,' he said. 'There's a queue of passengers waiting for me.'

'OK ... before you go 168 via Waterloo,' said Beatrice, 'I have something for you.' She took the lunch box out of her school bag and put the two portions of the delicious dessert right in front of his metal glazed mouth.

'It's a Tiramisu,' she announced.

'Tiramisu? How lovely!' the Bus exclaimed wolfing down both slices in no time.

'It was from Mr Cecco,' said Beatrice smiling, surprised by how quickly he had eaten them.

'My child, you have made my day,' replied 168 via Waterloo, feeling full and content, 'But let me ask you ... do you want to go on a talking bus tour of London, one day?'

Beatrice couldn't believe her ears. Did the Bus really ask her to go on a *talking bus tour* of London with him? But that was one of her dreams! Dream number 4, precisely.

'Yes! I'd love to!' she squealed with joy, still unsure if she was dreaming or not.

'I'll be your guide for the day,' the Bus

announced.

'Cool! But ... one day ... when ... 168 via Waterloo?' asked Beatrice.

'How about next Sunday? It's my only day off. We can meet here, right in front of Caramba Café. Ten o'clock sharp. I'll take you to see some of the most beautiful places in London.'

'Yes, yes! Thank you, 168 via Waterloo!'

Beatrice tried to hug him but her tiny arms only managed to reach a little part above the right wheel of the London Bus. It was enough though to make him blush and become four times redder than usual. The two friends said goodbye to each other with the promise of meeting up again the following Sunday.

Beatrice hardly ever got to go anywhere interesting. Now, she had a chance! Just like she had written down in her Dreams List!

Chapter Ten

TRICKY DAYS OF THE WEEK

'When is next Sunday exactly?' Beatrice said out loud. Beatrice was never any good at remembering which day of the week it was, for the very simple reason that she didn't think it was important. She picked up her diary, opened it — she was speechless!

'*Holly Crisps*! ... How many Mondays, Tuesdays, Wednesdays, Thursdays, Fridays, Saturdays and Sundays are in this diary? What a waste!' she sighed. 'I mean, are grown-ups crazy or what? I never realised they had come up with so many days of the week. OK, today is Thursday, May 27. Sunday is in three days!' she reasoned running her finger over the pages. 'Yes! There it is! Sunday May 30!'

On the Sunday May 30 page, Beatrice started writing VVSD, which meant Very, Very Special Day when suddenly, a powerful wind blew into the bedroom despite the fact that the window was shut. Then one after the other, some pages started flying out of her diary and turned into seven colourful water balloons.

They all had eyes, ears and mouths and were wearing a ribbon with a day of the week written on it.

'What's going on?' Beatrice exclaimed. She squinted her eyes, wrinkled her nose and scratched its tip, trying to figure out if what was happening was real or just her mind playing tricks on her.

At first, the days of the week ignored her and kept chatting to each other. Beatrice stared at them, waiting for something to happen when, completely out of the blue, one of the balloons said,

'Hello, Beatrice, sorry but you're making a big mistake. 'Don't write "VVSD" on the Sunday page.'

'And ... why not?'

Beatrice had been through so many mysterious happenings that talking to a day of the week didn't seem that strange to her anymore. She wondered how that day of the week knew her name.

'Because I am Sunday, although everyone thinks that I am Monday,' replied the balloon.

Baffled, Beatrice checked a Sunday page which read Sunday then the ribbon of the speaking balloon, which read Monday.

'Not again! How can you be Sunday if your ribbon says you are Monday?' she asked inquisitively. 'Monday must be thinking I'm really dumb,' she muttered under her breath, rolling her eyes.

While Beatrice was thinking what to do next, Tuesday, Wednesday and Thursday rushed towards her, all shouting they were Sunday too.

The only ones who kept drifting happily in the air were Friday, Saturday and Sunday himself.

Feeling frustrated, Beatrice dropped the diary on the floor. First the Maps of the World had tried to trick her, now the Days of the Week — she didn't really know what to think. All she wanted was for Sunday, May 30 to come so she could meet her newfound friend and go on a talking bus tour of London with him.

'Hello Beatrice, I can help you!' another balloon announced.

'Yeah right, how?'

'I am Saturday!'

'Oh at least you didn't say you were Sunday,' remarked Beatrice, 'Everyone else did.'

'My child, you should not believe Monday,

Tuesday, Wednesday and Thursday. I can tell you, they are not Sunday and Sunday is simply Sunday,' explained Saturday calmly.

'And why doesn't Sunday come out and say that for himself?' she asked, frowning.

'Because Sunday is very lazy — everyone knows that Sunday is a day when people like to rest or have fun. He just doesn't bother to come forward — that's also why the other days of the week are trying to be him. It's fun to be Sunday,' explained Saturday in a convincing voice.

'But ... what about you? Aren't you upset that you're not Sunday?' Beatrice asked suspiciously.

'Not at all! I am very happy to be Saturday thank you very much,' said the *balloon-day-of-the-week*. 'So is Friday. We are both happy days of the week. On Friday, people are thinking about the weekend and on Saturday, it's already the weekend!'

'Oh,' sighed Beatrice, trying to make sense of the crazy *days-of-the-week-conversation*.

'Then again, who would want to be Monday?' continued Saturday. 'It's the first day of the week, children have to go to school and grown-ups have to go to work.'

'I know, my mum always says that she hates Monday,' said Beatrice, looking at Saturday in a more trusting way. As soon as Monday heard all those bad things about him, he burst into a flood of tears.

'Oh, I am sorry Monday, please don't cry!' said Beatrice feeling sorry for him. 'I am actually very happy on Monday.'

'Why?' Monday asked, sobbing.

'Because on Monday I have Maths and since I don't like Maths, I pretend to be sick. My mum doesn't send me to school — I stay at home all day and play. Monday is fun!' said Beatrice empathetically, with a big smile on her face. Even if it had only happened once, Beatrice thought that a little white lie was OK to cheer Monday up.

'Thank you, Beatrice.' Monday wiped away his tears, blew his nose and finally smiled back, now very proud of his ribbon with his day of the week written on it. It was the very first time that someone had told him he was a FUN DAY. Pleased with Beatrice's story, all the other balloons deflated and slowly turned back into pages. Cheerfully dancing their way back into Beatrice's diary, they all waved goodbye even though they hadn't been told they were FUN DAYS.

Monday even blew her a kiss. Finally, Beatrice was able to write 'VVSD' in her diary, and on the right day — Sunday May 30. But hang on! *What if Sunday was every day and not just once a week? That would be nice,* she

thought. And she wrote Sunday on the other
May 29 page too, *just in case* Sunday May 30
page disappeared.

Chapter Eleven

VVSD,
A VERY, VERY
SPECIAL DAY

'Mark!' cried Beatrice grabbing her friend by the arm when she saw him at school at break time, the next day.

'Beatrice!'

'Sit down and hold tight! You won't believe what happened to me!'

'What? What *e-e-else* has *h-h-happened* to you?'

'OK, not only the Maps of the World talk but also the days of the week!'

'The days of the *w-w-week* talk? What did they *s-s-say*?'

'They argue more than talk. You should hear them! They argue like kids in a kindergarten. They babble all day long because they all want to be Sunday, apart from Friday and Saturday.'

'They are *r-r-right*. If I were a day of the week, I would like to be Sunday too. Sunday is *c-c-cool*. There's no *s-s-school* on Sunday and I don't do any homework.'

'That's right, everyone likes Sunday and guess what?'

'*W-w-what*?'

'OK, here's the news! I am going to go on a talking bus tour with my friend the London Bus!

'*A-a-are* you? When?'

'Next Sunday! He's going to drive me around London to show me many great places and new things!' she said, full of delight.

'*Wo-o-ow*,' Mark exclaimed, trying to be happy for his friend. He still could not believe Beatrice's incredible good luck. In fact, he had followed Beatrice's tip and had come up with a magic spell song too but nothing, absolutely nothing had happened. He had not bumped into a single talking thing — not even a bland, old, boring, chewed up pencil had said a word to him.

Poor Mark — he felt left out. He was about to ask Beatrice to take him with her on the talking bus tour, when she said,

'Mark, the Bus doesn't know that I told you he can talk. Please keep it a secret! OK?'

'OK, *I-I-I* will,' he mumbled, downhearted.

'I have to go back to my classroom now! I need to study the Map of London for my first talking bus tour with 168 via Waterloo — although, I think he knows the city quite well. See you later, Mark!'

'*S-s-see* you later Beatrice,' he replied in a sad voice.

'Oh Mark, I forgot! Can I say to my mum that I am coming to your place on Sunday?'

Mark nodded.

'Thank you! You're the best BFF!' Beatrice screeched, when finally she noticed Mark's dismay.

'I'll tell you everything when I am back, OK?'she said, smiling.

'OK,' Mark replied. He waved goodbye, watching his friend go.

'Am I still Beatrice's BFF?' he wondered, feeling sad.

***

'Mum, Mark has invited me to go to his place today and then we're going on a bus ride to Caramba Café. Can I go, please?' asked Beatrice when she woke up on her VVSD.

Mark lived very nearby.

'All right, but don't ask his parents and the bus driver too many questions. They might get annoyed,' her mum replied, her eyes firmly fixed on a fitness and yoga magazine.

'OK, I won't bother them,' Beatrice had a cheeky glint in her eye, which her mother might have noticed if she had lifted her nose a fraction out of the pages.

Instead, Beatrice headed to Caramba Café to meet her London Bus friend. You could hear her humming her little magic spell song as she walked down the footpath.

'Hello, 168 via Waterloo, you look great!' she said joyfully as soon as she spotted him.

The London Bus looked much cleaner and redder.

'Thank you, my dear,' he replied. 'It's the weekend! You see, I always get a sponge bath on a Sunday.'

'It makes you really shine,' Beatrice said, gazing at him in admiration.

'Well, get on board, young lady,' commanded the London Bus. 'Let's go!'

Beatrice hopped on the 168 via Waterloo and took a seat at the back.

'Oh no, you must take the driver's seat Beatrice,' said the London Bus. 'Don't worry, I'll help with the driving,' he reassured her.

'Oh! Thank you, thank you!' Beatrice shrieked, astonished. She jumped into the driver's seat and noticed a picture of Pepe, the missing ginger cat, hanging just above the seat. The cat was wearing a driver's hat.

Beatrice had the impression that Pepe had just winked at her, showing off his most charming cat-grin.

'Hello Pepe!' she whispered winking back at him. Then she turned around and looked at the road ahead.

It was the first time Beatrice had sat in the driver's seat of a London Bus. The seat was very large and incredibly comfortable.

Beatrice grabbed the steering wheel and, looking at it ecstatically, she said,

'168 via Waterloo, may I ask you a question?'

'Speak now or forever hold your peace,

child!'

'OK, I'll speak now. Does that mean that I am —' she hesitated, 'does that mean that I am ... a ... a ... bus driver?' she asked, trembling like a leaf. Her legs felt like jelly. Beatrice could hardly believe that she didn't even have to wait to grow up for dream number 1 to come true.

'If it looks like a duck, swims like a duck, and quacks like a duck then it probably is a duck! You are not a duck, my dear, but you are indeed a bus driver. A Routemaster Bus Driver precisely!'

Beatrice was over the moon. In the few weeks since she had seen that model bus in the shop, four of her top dreams had, astonishingly, come true. And that was not all — Beatrice had also learned many new things about grown-ups. For example, that not all of them were boring, weird, messed up in the head or confused.

Miss Pauline and Mr Cecco certainly were not, and that was because they were able to listen, help and explain things even to a little girl like her who was always getting tangled up with words and was always compared to a *buzzing fly,* or even worse, to an *annoying ugly fly.*

She had finally realised that school didn't completely 'suck'.

She had met her best friend forever there — Mark, the best BFF. Sadly, he could not go on the talking bus tour with her because 168 via Waterloo had told her not to tell anyone that he was a talking bus — even though she had already told Mark everything.

Above all, she was beaming with happiness because she had been able to find the very famous London Bus, *168 via Waterloo, the last Routemaster in the world, who's only friends with the brave and the bold.*

Together, they were now embarking on the greatest adventure of her life — driving around London and visiting the centre of the city, finally making dream number 4 come true.

With her special hairband on, Beatrice looked the part completely — a real bus driver in the making! She was really proud of herself.

'I'm ready!' she announced from the driver's seat.

Wearing his usual bowler hat, a sign at the back which read, 'Sunday: Routemasters' lazy day, no pictures, no rides!' and a silver spoon hanging from a hook next to his glazed left eye — a present from Mr Cecco — 168 via Waterloo started up his front-mounted engine, producing a loud popping, cracking sound. The real Annoying, Ugly, Fly — that's what we will call her from now on since no one in London knows her real name — followed them and buzzed into the bus through the open rear platform.

She flew so fast that she crashed against the opposite window and dropped into one of the seats. Neither Beatrice nor the Routemaster Bus noticed her though.

Carrying Beatrice, the Annoying, Ugly, Fly and the picture of Pepe on board, the old Bus made his way towards the centre of London on a beautiful sunny, lazy VVSD.

'I love this VVSD!' Beatrice said smiling.

'VVSD? What does that mean?' asked 168 via Waterloo.

'VVSD means, Very, Very, Special Day. Today!'

'I love this VVSD too! London, here we come!' the London Bus announced, roaring like a lion and swelling with pride.

Beatrice could hardly believe that she was "driving" a real LONDON BUS! Another of her dreams had come true, despite everything and despite everyone. She was ready to go. Bye-bye Belsize Park. Bye-bye old life! The adventures of Beatrice and the London Bus in London had only just begun. But, hang on a moment! Will Beatrice say bye-bye to Mark too?

THIS IS NOT
THE END!

NO!
NOT AT ALL
THE END!

... BECAUSE ...

... more fun awaits you in the next book! Our two friends meet every Sunday, and the London Bus, Routemaster 168 via Waterloo introduces Beatrice to a mysterious, secret and mesmerising city packed with nutty, dreamy, sloppy, moaning famous talking buildings, babbling and big-headed tourist attractions, strange creatures and some complicated VIGs (Very Important Grown-ups).

This is a world full of SECRETS, which have been kept guarded for a very long time.
Soon Beatrice learns that London is not the city everyone — inhabitants and tourists alike — thinks it is.

Beatrice and the London Bus - The Secrets of London is the only book in London, in the United Kingdom and in the entire world, including the universe, where these incredible secrets are revealed. Grab it now before it's too late!

BUT REMEMBER! Once you've read it, don't spill the beans! These secrets are meant to stay forever a SECRET!

The World's Best Spelling Author

Francesca Lombardo

The Book Series!
GET THE NEXT BOOK!

Get the next book!

Now that you've read the first book, grab the next book of the series – volume two – and step into a world packed with secrets and exciting adventures! If you wish to write to the author, send an email to:

author@dailyfairytales.co.uk

www.beatriceandthelondonbus.co.uk

Get the

LONDON MAP,
and play the

LONDON TOUR GUIDE GAME!

www.beatriceandthelondonbus.co.uk/
the-london-map/

Get the
LONDON MAP
COLOURING BOOK
Available from and AMAZON!!

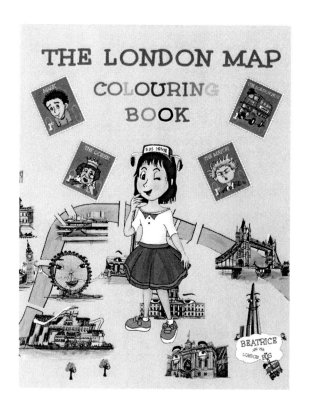

www.beatriceandthelondonbus.co.uk/
beatrice-store/

Visit **London** with the special

BEATRICE
AND
THE LONDON BUS
TOUR!

www.beatriceandthelondonbus.co.uk/
the-london-bus-tour/

Enter
THE DRAWING
COMPETITION!

Send your artwork inspired by the stories and illustrations of Beatrice and the London Bus book series to competitions@dailyfairytales.co.uk

THE PRIZE IS A SURPRISE!

www.beatriceandthelondonbus.co.uk/ competitions/

143

Lightning Source UK Ltd.
Milton Keynes UK
UKOW01f0708130516

274177UK00001B/4/P